Will It Rain?

by HOLLY KELLER

GREENWILLOW BOOKS  NEW YORK

TO NOËLLA,
FOR SO MANY THINGS

Greenwillow Books,
a division of
William Morrow
& Company, Inc.,
105 Madison Avenue,
New York, N.Y. 10016.
Printed in the
United States
of America
First Edition

10 9 8 7 6 5 4 3 2 1

Library of Congress
Cataloging in Publication Data

Keller, Holly.
Will it rain?

Summary:
When the clouds darken
and the wind hums and
blows, all the animals
living in and around
the pond wonder if
it will rain.
[1. Rain and rainfall
—Fiction.
2. Animals—Fiction]
I. Title.
PZ7.K28132Wi   1984
[E]   83-25423
ISBN 0-688-03839-5
ISBN 0-688-03840-9 (lib. bdg.)

Robin was pulling on a fat worm
when he felt the change.
Squirrel noticed it too.
He sniffed the air.

A chilly breeze rushed through
the tall grass where Mouse
was playing.

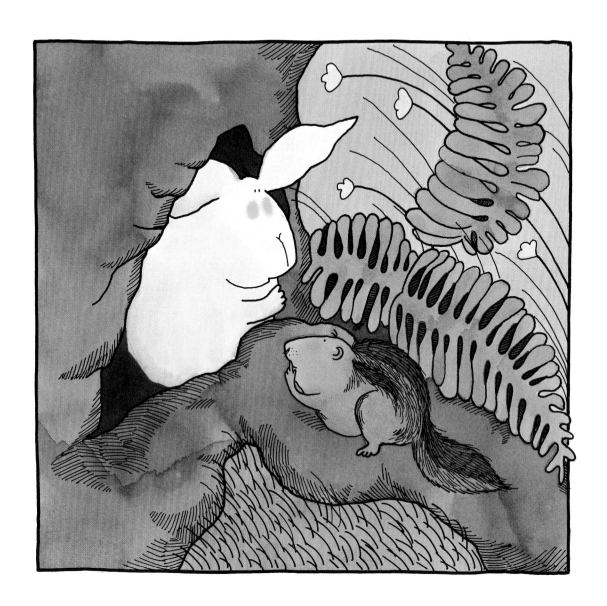

Black clouds darkened the sky.
"Will it rain?" Rabbit asked.
"Be still and listen," Chipmunk said.

The wind was getting louder.
It made a humming sound.
It blew the leaves upside down.

It blew the sparrows
out of the hemlock.

It blew across the pond, making
ripples. It blew Goose and Duck into
the cattails. Frog croaked loudly
and disappeared under the water.

"Will it rain?" Mouse asked.
Rabbit hurried inside.

Chipmunk ran up the tree
to Squirrel's branch.

Mouse wriggled under a fern.

A great crash shook the tree.

Lightning streaked across the sky.

The noise woke Skunk and Possum.
Robin felt the first drop on
his tail. "It's coming," he said.

The rain began to fall faster and harder.
It pounded on the ground.

It splashed in the pond.
It slapped against the tree.
It made big puddles in the yard
and little rivers in the garden.

Chipmunk pushed into Squirrel's hole.
Mouse squeezed his eyes shut
and covered his ears.

Then suddenly it was quiet.

Mist hung over the pond.
The grass glistened and
the air felt warm again.

Rabbit popped out of his hole.
Mouse opened his eyes.

Squirrel and Chipmunk ran down
the tree. Robin began to sing.

Goose and Duck swam in circles
around the pond.

The sparrows came back
to the hemlock.

And the sun came out.